Wolf

Who Kidnapped the Mayor?

Roderick Hunt
Illustrated by Alex Brychta

OXFORD
UNIVERSITY PRESS

OXFORD
UNIVERSITY PRESS

Great Clarendon Street, Oxford OX2 6DP

Oxford University Press is a department of the University of Oxford.
It furthers the University's objective of excellence in research, scholarship,
and education by publishing worldwide in

Oxford New York

Auckland Cape Town Dar es Salaam Hong Kong Karachi
Kuala Lumpur Madrid Melbourne Mexico City Nairobi
New Delhi Shanghai Taipei Toronto

With offices in

Argentina Austria Brazil Chile Czech Republic France Greece
Guatemala Hungary Italy Japan Poland Portugal Singapore
South Korea Switzerland Thailand Turkey Ukraine Vietnam

Oxford is a registered trade mark of Oxford University Press
in the UK and in certain other countries

© text Roderick Hunt 2000
© illustrations Alex Brychta

The moral rights of the author have been asserted

Database right Oxford University Press (maker)

First published 2000

All rights reserved. No part of this publication may be reproduced,
stored in a retrieval system, or transmitted, in any form or by any means,
without the prior permission in writing of Oxford University Press,
or as expressly permitted by law, or under terms agreed with the appropriate
reprographics rights organization. Enquiries concerning reproduction
outside the scope of the above should be sent to the Rights Department,
Oxford University Press, at the address above

You must not circulate this book in any other binding or cover
and you must impose this same condition on any acquirer

British Library Cataloguing in Publication Data

Data available

ISBN-13: 978 0 19 918756 0
ISBN-10: 0-19-918756-8

10 9

Printed in Hong Kong

Chapter 1

Loz and Gran stared at the man in amazement. He was right on the edge of Gran's allotment. In his hand was a red and white pole.

'A bit more to the right,' yelled a voice.

The man stepped sideways on to Gran's seed bed.

'Hey!' shouted Gran angrily. 'What are you doing? I've planted seeds just there.'

Loz looked across the allotment. A woman was looking through something like a camera on a tripod. The woman wrote on a clip-board. Then she waved at the man.

'Now move back about ten metres,' she shouted.

The man looked at Gran. He tried to scuff out his footprints in the freshly dug earth.

'I'm sorry about your seed bed,' he said.

'What are you doing?' asked Gran. 'And why do you need to trample over people's gardens?'

'It's a survey,' said the man.

'A survey!' exclaimed Gran. 'What

survey? Why are you doing it on our allotments?'

The man looked shifty. 'I don't know,' he said. 'I only hold the pole.'

'Right!' said Gran. 'I'll ask someone who might know.'

She marched across to the woman. Loz followed. 'What's this survey all about?' she demanded.

'I'm afraid I'm not allowed to say,' said the woman.

Gran looked at Loz. 'I don't like the sound of this,' she said. 'Something fishy is going on.'

Chapter 2

That afternoon Loz met Najma and they walked up Wolf Street together.

A car was parked outside Kat's house. Kat was standing beside it.

'What a great set of wheels!' said Najma. 'Whose car is it?'

'It belongs to my cousin, Phil,' replied Kat.

Phil came out of the house. He waved goodbye to Mrs Wilson. Then he walked towards the car rattling the keys in his hand.

Phil grinned at Loz and Najma. He spun the keys round on his finger and put on an American accent. 'OK, you Guys,' he said. 'This is Phil "The Ace" Wilson. I'm looking for a front-page news story.'

Loz and Najma looked blank.

Kat smiled. 'He's got a job, that's all.'

'What sort of job?' asked Loz.

'Meet your star reporter for the local newspaper,' said Phil. 'I am now a key member of the Wolf Hill Gazette.'

'Ignore him,' laughed Kat. 'He's doing work experience, that's all. It's part of his college course.'

'But they will let me write some news,' said Phil, 'if I can find a story to report. And if it's good enough.'

Loz looked thoughtful. 'I may have a story for you,' she said.

She told Phil about the people on the allotments. 'They were doing a survey, but they refused to tell Gran why.'

'Maybe they are searching for oil,' said Phil. 'I guess they will start drilling any day. I can see the headline, "Oil well found on Gran's Patch".'

'It's not funny,' said Loz. 'Gran loves that allotment.'

Chapter 3

The drilling started on Monday morning. Loz could hardly believe it. She ran to find Kat and Najma.

She found them sitting on the edge of the school field talking to Chris.

'Come quickly!' gasped Loz. 'They are drilling for oil. There's a drill in

the allotments. That wasn't a joke about looking for oil. Come and see!'

They all ran to the end of the school field. The allotments were on the other side of a high fence. The four of them peered through the links of the fence.

A lorry had driven down the little lane beside it. On the back of the lorry was a thing like a tall crane.

But it was not a crane. It was a machine that drilled a long, thin, steel tube into the ground.

Some people were standing round the drill. They were wearing hard hats. One of them was the woman that Loz had seen doing the survey.

'Phil's joke about drilling for oil,' said Loz. 'It wasn't a joke after all.'

'They can't be looking for oil,' said Chris. 'There must be another reason.'

Chris was right. There was another reason – and it was far worse than any of them could have imagined.

Chapter 4

Kat, Loz, Chris and Najma stared at Phil.

'They're going to *close* Wolf Hill School!' they gasped.

'It's true, I tell you,' said Phil. 'It's a really big story. Wait until you see the newspaper tomorrow.'

Mrs Wilson frowned. 'Start again, Phil,' she said. 'I mean you must have got this all wrong. Why would they want to close Wolf Hill School?'

'It's the new Traffic Relief Scheme,' said Phil. 'It's just a proposal at the moment. They want to build an inner-city relief road. If it goes ahead, the road will come along the canal. Then it will go across the allotments.'

'But what's this about a flyover?' asked Kat.

'The new road will cross Wolf Hill Road as a flyover. It will need slip roads to get on and off it. One of the slip roads will go across the school field and the allotments.'

'So that's why they were drilling,' said Loz.

'That's right,' said Phil. 'The drilling was part of a survey to see if a new road could be built there.'

Chris looked puzzled. 'But why will

they close the school?' he asked.

'The plan is to widen Wolf Hill Road,' went on Phil. 'They'll use the land along the side of the school.'

'So what will happen to us if the school is closed?' asked Kat.

'Wolf Hill would merge with Lark Field School,' said Phil. 'Lark Field has plenty of room.'

'Lark Field! That's terrible!' shouted Najma. 'I'd hate to go there.'

'Well, the plans are just a proposal,' said Phil. 'There will be an enquiry about it.'

'And a protest,' said Mrs Wilson. 'We protested once before about a factory; and we won! We'll have to protest again.'

Chapter 5

The chanting began in one part of the hall. 'No road here! No road here!' More and more people joined in. The noise grew louder and louder. 'No road here! NO ROAD HERE!'

Loz and Najma felt quite scared. It seemed odd to hear grown-ups chanting in the school hall. A man in

a grey suit stood next to Mr Saffrey. He had a huge map of Wolf Hill. The new road could be seen on the map.

Mr Saffrey held up his hands. 'Please! Please!' he shouted. 'We all want to hear the proposals for the Traffic Relief Scheme.'

Najma looked at the man in the suit. Next to him was the Mayor, and beside him was a tall woman. Najma stared at her. She thought she had seen the woman before. But where?

The chanting went on. Some people began to stamp on the floor. 'Please! Quiet, everyone,' shouted Mr Saffrey.

‘Thank you!’ said Mr Saffrey. ‘Now I want to introduce Mr Ford from the Council.’

Mr Ford cleared his throat and began. ‘We need a relief road. Our streets are congested. There are just too many cars,’ he said. ‘Traffic is so bad that we have to do something. One day last summer, the town came to a standstill.’

Mr Ford pointed to the map. He showed them where the road would go. It would cover most of the school field. This would mean closing down Wolf Hill School.

‘What happens to the children if the school is shut?’ shouted a man.

Mr Ford mopped his forehead. ‘Well, the children will transfer to Lark Field School. It is quite close.

And the school has plenty of room.'

'But it's on the other side of a busy road,' put in Mrs Wilson.

'We'd have a crossing attendant,' said Mr Ford.

Mr Wilson stood up. 'The new road crosses Wolf Hill Park. What will happen to the football club?'

'The road will go close to the club, but not through the ground,' said Mr Ford.

'What about the allotments?' asked Gran. 'Some of us have had an allotment for years.'

'We will be able to put new allotments on what's left of the school field,' said Mr Ford.

Gran whispered to Najma's Mum. 'I don't like the sound of it. This man has an answer for everything.'

Chapter 6

Gran and Loz stood on the street corner. They had a table and a poster saying 'Save Our School'.

'Sign our petition,' called Gran, waving a sheet of paper.

Mrs Wilson joined them. 'Time for me to take over,' she said.

'It's hard work,' said Gran. 'Most people agree with us, but not everyone wants to sign. Some people say we need the relief road.'

Later that day, Loz was in the den with Najma, Chris, and Kat. Loz was talking about the petition. 'Some people wouldn't sign it,' she said. 'They say we need the relief road.'

'But we don't want a big, fast road close to where we live,' said Najma.

'And we don't want our school closed down,' put in Loz.

Just then, someone came down the steps of the den. It was Phil. He looked pleased.

'I thought I would find you here,' he said. 'I'm going to write my first piece for the newspaper. It's an interview with the Mayor about the relief road. I need to think of some good questions to ask him.' He waved a brand new notebook in front of them.

'Well, is the Mayor against the new road, or is he for it?' asked Loz.

'I don't know,' said Phil. 'That's what I'll find out.'

'What Phil needs is a really big story,' said Najma. 'Interviews are all very well, but . . .'

'Najma's right,' said Phil. 'I need something to hit the headlines.'

'Like what?' asked Chris. Everyone looked blank.

'We could kidnap the Mayor,' laughed Kat. 'Phil shouldn't interview him, he should kidnap him! Then he can write about it for the paper. It would make a great headline. "Wolf Hill Mayor in Kidnap Drama!" '

'Kidnap the Mayor! Don't be silly,' said Najma. 'We could never do a thing like that?'

'It was a joke,' said Kat.

Phil looked thoughtful. 'But we could,' he said, 'if the Mayor agreed to it.'

Everyone stared at him.

'Why would he agree to a thing like that?' said Chris. 'It's a crazy idea.'

'Publicity,' said Phil. 'Think what a good story it would make. If the Mayor is against the road he might let himself be kidnapped. It would be great publicity for the protest. It might be a way to help save the school.'

'But Chris is right,' said Kat. 'The Mayor would never agree to it.'

'There's one way to find out,' said Phil.

'How?' asked Loz.

'I'll ask him,' said Phil.

Chapter 7

A crowd waited outside a new supermarket. A black car pulled up. Inside was the Mayor and his wife. They stepped out and walked towards the supermarket doors.

Najma saw someone else get out of the car – the tall woman who had been at the meeting. Najma stared at her. If only she could remember where she had seen her before.

A man stepped forward to welcome them. The Mayor opened the supermarket. Cameras flashed.

Suddenly an old, white car raced up. It screeched to a halt. Two men leaped out and ran towards the Mayor. They grabbed him by the arms.

It was all over in a flash. One of the men shouted, 'Keep back!' while the others dragged the Mayor to the white car and pushed him inside. Blue smoke rose from the tyres as the car screeched off.

Phil watched it speed away. 'Brilliant!' he said. He turned to the photographer beside him.

'Did you get good pictures?' he asked.

The photographer grinned. 'I sure did!' he said.

'Right,' said Phil. 'Let's go. I've got a story to write up.'

. . . . .

That evening, Kat looked in the Wolf Hill Gazette.

'Here it is!' she exclaimed.

'What is?' asked Mrs Wilson.

'Phil's story about the Mayor being kidnapped,' replied Kat. She read out loud: ' "Mayor in Road Protest Kidnap Drama". It was a drama, too,' she added.

Mrs Wilson took the paper and read the story.

'Why would anyone want to kidnap the Mayor? I wonder who did it?' she said.

Kat grinned. She knew who had done it - Phil's friends. It seemed amazing to think the Mayor had agreed to it. But he had. She even knew where they had taken the Mayor, but that was a secret.

Chapter 8

The next day, the gang was in the school playground. Kat, Loz, Chris, and Najma were excited.

'It was our idea,' said Loz, proudly. 'We thought of the kidnap.'

At the same time a police car stopped outside the school gates . . .

'It was great,' said Najma. 'The Mayor pretended to look really surprised.'

'You would never have guessed he knew all about it,' laughed Kat.

Two police officers got out of the car, and went into the school . . .

'Phil was right,' said Loz. 'It was a great publicity stunt. People will get to hear about the protest and sign the petition to save the school.'

The policemen spoke to Mr Saffrey . . .

Chris looked at Kat. 'What happened to the Mayor after he was snatched?' he asked.

The police officers walked across the playground. Mr Saffrey walked between them . . .

'He went to Mr Saffrey's house,'

said Kat. 'Mr Saffrey put him up for the night.'

'Mr Saffrey!' exclaimed Loz. 'How on earth did he get involved?'

'Phil talked him into it,' replied Kat.

One of the police officers held Mr Saffrey's arm . . .

'I can't imagine Mr Saffrey kidnapping anyone,' said Loz.

The police officers went to their car. They took Mr Saffrey.

'Nor can I,' said Kat, 'but he said he'd do anything to save the school.'

'You know Mr Saffrey,' said Najma. 'He loves this school.'

Mr Saffrey got into the back of the police car. A police officer got in beside him. There was a worried look on Mr Saffrey's face . . .

The school bell rang. 'Lunch break over,' said Chris. 'Time to go in.'

The police car drove away.

Chapter 9

Inspector Webb looked at Mr Saffrey. 'You do see how serious this is?' she said. 'Kidnapping is a criminal offence.'

Mr Saffrey frowned. 'But it wasn't a real kidnap. It was a publicity stunt.'

'What do you mean, a publicity stunt?' asked the Inspector.

'It wasn't serious,' said Mr Saffrey. 'It was a protest about closing the school. The Mayor was in on it. He agreed to the whole thing. Ask his wife. She will tell you.'

'We did,' said the Inspector. 'She says she knew nothing about it. The kidnapping was a complete shock.'

Mr Saffrey gasped. 'But that can't be true,' he said.

'So I'll ask you again,' said the Inspector. 'Where is the Mayor now, exactly?'

'How would I know?' replied Mr Saffrey. 'I told you. He stayed the night in my house. He had breakfast. After that, I guess he went home.'

'But the Mayor is missing,' said Inspector Webb. 'His wife is worried. She says she hasn't heard from him.

Nobody has seen him. So where is he?'

'I'm afraid I've no idea,' said Mr Saffrey.

The Inspector put a tape recorder on her desk. 'We received this tape at eleven o'clock this morning.' She pressed the play button.

The recording was of the Mayor. He spoke in a strained voice. *'I've been kidnapped . . . I don't know where I'm being held . . . I have a blindfold on . . . I'm telling you, this isn't a joke . . .'*

The Inspector switched off the recorder.

'But this is crazy,' said Mr Saffrey. 'I know nothing about this. I only know what the Mayor agreed to let us do.'

The Inspector's face was grim. 'This is how I see it,' she said. 'The Mayor has been kidnapped. He is still being held somewhere. You say you know nothing about this, but you are involved in the kidnap.'

Mr Saffrey shook his head. 'It was just a silly stunt,' he said.

'It may be a stunt,' said the Inspector, 'but I have to take it seriously. I'm sorry. I'm going to have to keep you here for now.'

Mr Saffrey gulped. 'You mean, I'm under arrest?'

'Let's say you are helping us with our enquiries,' said Inspector Webb.

Mr Saffrey's voice shook. 'Do you think I could phone the school? I'm due to take a games lesson in five minutes.'

Chapter 10

'Mr Saffrey arrested! I just can't believe it,' said Nan. She shook her head and repeated, 'Mr Saffrey arrested. Whatever can he have done?'

Loz's Nan was one of the school cleaners. Every so often, Nan worked late. She had to treat the hall floor with non-slip polish. It was a big job.

Loz sometimes stayed behind and helped her.

'It was all about that kidnapping,' said Loz. 'You know, outside that store, yesterday.'

Just then Loz looked out of the window. She thought she saw a woman in the playground. She went to the window and looked out. There was no one to be seen.

‘That’s funny!’ said Loz ‘I thought I saw someone out there. I must have imagined it.’

‘I wonder if it will be in this evening’s paper?’ asked Nan.

‘What?’ replied Loz.

‘The arrest of Mr Saffrey,’ said Nan.

‘Why not buy a paper on the way home?’ said Loz.

. . . . .

Phil looked upset. Kat’s mum put her hand on his shoulder.

‘How long were you at the police station?’ asked Kat.

‘All day,’ said Phil. ‘They kept asking the same question – “What have you done with the Mayor?”

They think I know where he is.'

'I don't understand,' said Mrs Wilson. 'How could a fake kidnap turn into the real one?'

'I don't know,' replied Phil. 'It's a nightmare.' He picked up the paper. 'We got publicity all right: "Kidnap Mystery Deepens".'

He read on: 'The whereabouts of the kidnapped Mayor of Wolf Hill remains a mystery. Today police questioned Mr Richard Saffrey, Head Teacher of Wolf Hill School . . .'

'Poor Mr Saffrey,' said Mrs Wilson. 'You don't think he's behind it, do you?'

There was a knock on the door. It was Loz and Nan. Nan had a copy of the newspaper. 'Have you seen this?' she asked.

'You'd better come in,' said Mrs Wilson.

. . . .

Later that evening, Inspector Webb called at Nan's house.

'Mrs Smith?' she asked. 'I believe

you are a key holder for Wolf Hill School?'

'That's right,' said Nan. 'I do have keys to the school. I lock up each evening.'

'We need to search the school,' said Inspector Webb. 'We'd like you to come and unlock it.'

'There's nothing wrong, is there?' asked Nan.

'We don't know, yet,' replied Inspector Webb.

'All right,' said Nan. 'I'll get the keys. But I'll have to bring Loz. She's my granddaughter. I can't leave her alone in the house.'

So Loz went to the school with Nan and the Inspector. Nan unlocked the door and they went inside. 'The intruder alarm is still set,' said Nan. 'No one has broken in.'

They looked round the school but they found nothing.

'Are there any sheds or buildings outside?' asked Inspector Webb.

'Only the games store,' said Nan. 'It's a big shed.'

'We'll take a look anyway,' said

Inspector Webb.

They went outside and Nan unlocked the shed. The door swung open. Nan gasped in surprise and jumped back. 'My goodness!' she exclaimed.

The Mayor was in the shed. He was tied to an old chair. He had a piece of sticky tape over his mouth.

Chapter 11

'The school got publicity all right,' said Najma. 'Bad publicity.'

The friends were in the den. Kat had a copy of the latest newspaper.

'Read it again,' asked Chris.

Najma read aloud. 'Mayor Slams Reckless Head.'

Najma read on. 'A Head Teacher was today condemned for a reckless stunt. Richard Saffrey (41) was behind Thursday's kidnapping of Wolf Hill Mayor.'

'I can't believe Mr Saffrey would take it so far,' said Chris.

'The Mayor was snatched by two men and held for thirty-two hours against his will. Police rescued him last night at Wolf Hill School. "It was a terrifying experience," said the Mayor. "I was tied to a chair . . .".'

'Oh no! Listen to this,' went on Najma: 'The Mayor condemned Mr Saffrey, saying that the kidnapping was an irresponsible stunt. He said that Saffrey got the idea from some Year Six pupils. He asked if Saffrey was fit to be in charge of a school.'

'It looks really bad,' said Chris. 'You don't think they'd sack Mr Saffrey, do you?'

'If they did, it would be easier to close the school down,' said Najma.

'This is so depressing,' said Kat.

So far Loz had been silent. Then she said, 'I've been thinking about something.'

'What?' asked Najma.

'Someone had to tie up the Mayor and lock him in the games shed,' said Loz. 'Who was it?'

'What do you mean?' asked Chris.

'Well, what if the Mayor was behind his own kidnap,' said Loz. 'What if he secretly wants the relief road?'

'Then why not just say so?' said Kat. 'Lots of people do want the new road.'

'Yesterday I stayed late at school to help Nan,' went on Loz. 'I couldn't be sure, but I thought I saw someone in the playground.'

'Who?' asked Kat.

'I think it was a woman,' said Loz. 'I'd seen her before. She's quite tall. You often see her with the Mayor. I think she might work for him. She could be his secretary.'

'Even if it was his secretary, we can't prove any of this,' said Chris.

Suddenly Najma gasped. 'Maybe we can prove it,' she said.

Everyone stared at her.

'This tall woman – the Mayor's secretary,' said Najma excitedly. 'I've been trying to think where I've seen her before. Now I remember. All we need is a good picture of her.'

'Phil might have a picture of her,' said Kat.

'Come on, let's find him,' said Najma.

Phil had several pictures of the kidnapping. He had them in a folder. One of them was a picture of the Mayor's secretary.

'It's quite a good photograph,' he said. 'It was taken just before the kidnap took place.'

'Do you mind if we borrow it?' asked Najma.

'No,' said Phil. 'It's no use to me any more. The Wolf Hill Gazette wouldn't keep me on after the kidnap affair.'

'I'm sorry,' said Kat.

Chapter 12

Everyone went to Najma's house. They all crowded round her computer. The screen showed the face of the Mayor's secretary. Najma clicked on the mouse.

'I've scanned in the picture,' she explained. 'It's in a program called Makeover Plus. You can use it to change someone's face. I'll start by changing the hair.'

She clicked on an icon. The screen showed lots of hairstyles – like little wigs.

'I need to change her long blonde hair,' said Najma.

She clicked on a short, dark wig. The hair was straight with a fringe.

Then she placed it on the picture of the woman.

'Right!' said Najma. 'I'll just remove her glasses . . .'

Chris gasped. 'That's amazing, Najma. Now I see who it is! That's the woman who wanted to buy old Archie's place. You remember her. She wanted to throw Archie off his land and build a factory on it.'

'I remember her!' said Kat. 'Mr Saffrey led that protest march against the factory.'

'It was a great protest!' said Loz. 'Archie threw eggs at her.'

'So why has she changed her appearance?' asked Najma. 'What's behind all this?'

'It's the relief road. There must be something in it for her,' said Chris. 'Perhaps she can make money out of the new road.'

'But what can we do now?' said Kat. 'Even if we do know who she is?'

'We can tell Mr Saffrey,' said Najma.

'I know someone else who would listen to us,' said Loz. 'Inspector Webb.'

Conclusion

The woman looked at the Mayor. Her eyes flashed angrily. 'Pull yourself together,' she said.

'But Saffrey will get the sack. He's a good man. I didn't mean things to go so far,' replied the Mayor.

'I've spent months setting this up,' went on the woman. 'We both stand to make a lot of money. You can't get cold feet now.'

There was a knock on the door.

'Come in,' called the Mayor.

Inspector Webb entered the room. 'I'd like to ask you both a few questions,' she said.

. . . . .

'So, it turns out that the Mayor and his secretary are crooks, then?' said Kat.

'They are,' replied Inspector Webb. 'They bought all the old factories along the canal. And they bought houses on the other side of Wolf Hill Road.'

'But why?' asked Chris. 'That's where the road might have gone.'

'That was the idea,' explained the Inspector. 'They bought all the property cheaply. Then they could sell it for a much higher price to the road builders. They stood to make a fortune.'

'So they used my kidnapping idea to try and make Mr Saffrey look bad,' said Phil.

'What about this tall woman?' asked Loz.

'She was behind it all. First, she changed her appearance. Then she began to work for the Mayor. That's how she got him involved.'

'Quiet, everyone,' called Mrs Wilson. 'Here's Mr Saffrey.'

Mr Saffrey walked into the hall.

Everyone cheered. Then they began to sing 'For he's a jolly good fellow.'

Someone shouted 'Speech!'

Mr Saffrey looked surprised. 'Thank you, everyone,' he said. 'This is a wonderful moment for me. It's great not to be under suspicion of kidnapping.'

Everyone laughed and cheered again.

'Thanks to Inspector Webb's investigation,' he went on, 'the school is safe and the relief road won't be built through Wolf Hill.'

The Inspector looked pleased.

'We have to thank Najma and her friends,' she said. 'It is because of them that we uncovered a big fraud. As you know, the plans for a road have been scrapped.'

'I've just had a thought,' said Chris. 'Next year we'll all be at the High School. We won't be at Wolf Hill School. Why did we bother to help save it?'

'Get him!' shouted Loz. They all grabbed him.

'Gerroff!' yelled Chris. 'I was only joking.'

Level 1

The Hole in the Ground
Hidden Gold
The Flying Armchair
I Hate Computers!
The Night it Rained Chips
Toxic Waste

More Level 1

People Like That
Andy the Hero
Fair Scare
It Can't Be
Blaze!
A Good Tip

Level 2

Funny Sort of Treasure
Arjo's Bike
In the Net
Million-Dollar Egg
The Exploding Parrot
The Pool Party

Level 3

Siren Green
Remote Control
Blazing Burgers
Skydive Wedding
Electric Sandwiches
Copper Cockerel

Level 4

Who's Kooza?
Ghost
In the End
Let's Hear It for Nan
Hostage!
Dirt Bike Rider

Level 5

Black Holme Island
Who Kidnapped the Mayor?
Scottish Adventure
Alien
Sleepover Shock
Last Term at Wolf Hill